That's Where God Is

Dan & Ali Morrow

Illustrated by Cory Godbey

David C Cook®
transforming lives together
www.davidccook.com

THAT'S WHERE GOD IS
Published by David C Cook
4050 Lee Vance View
Colorado Springs, CO 80918 U.S.A.

David C Cook Distribution Canada
55 Woodslee Avenue, Paris, Ontario, Canada N3L 3E5

David C Cook U.K., Kingsway Communications
Eastbourne, East Sussex BN23 6NT, England

The graphic circle C logo is a registered trademark of David C Cook.

LCCN 2010924062
ISBN 978-1-4347-6434-8
eISBN 978-1-4347-0222-7

© 2010 Daniel Morrow and Alison Strobel Morrow
The author is represented by MacGregor Literary.

The Team: Don Pape, Jean C. Fischer, Amy Kiechlin, Caitlyn York, Karen Athen
Cover and interior illustrations: Cory Godbey

Manufactured in Shen Zhen, Guang Dong, P.R. China, in May 2014 by Printplus Limited.
First Edition 2010

2 3 4 5 6 7 8 9 10

042914

For Abby Joy and Penny Jane,

in whom we see God every day

On Sundays I go to Grandpa's house. He picks me up,
swings me around, and together we fall into his big comfy
chair. We talk about all sorts of things. One day I asked
him, "Grandpa, where is God?"

"That's a good question!" Grandpa said. "Why don't you
look for Him this week? Then, next Sunday you can tell me
where He is."

I wasn't sure where to look, but I told Grandpa I would try.

He gave me a big hug and said, "Keep your eyes open.

I'm sure you'll find God all over the place."

On Monday my class went to the zoo. We saw elephants, giraffes, monkeys, and my favorite, a lion. My teacher says that God made all the animals. *That's where God is!* I thought. He's at the zoo with the animals He made.

Genesis 1:25

God made all kinds of wild animals. He made all kinds of livestock. He made all kinds of creatures that move along the ground. And God saw that it was good.

On Tuesday we went for ice cream. Before I'd even tasted mine, one scoop fell off my cone and smashed onto the ground. "No problem!" said my sister, Penny. "You can have some of mine." *That's where God is!* I thought. He's with us when we share.

Hebrews 13:16

Don't forget to do good. Don't forget to share with others. God is pleased with those kinds of offerings.

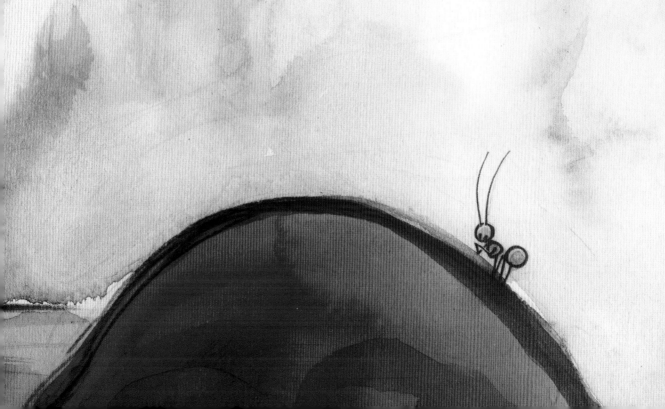

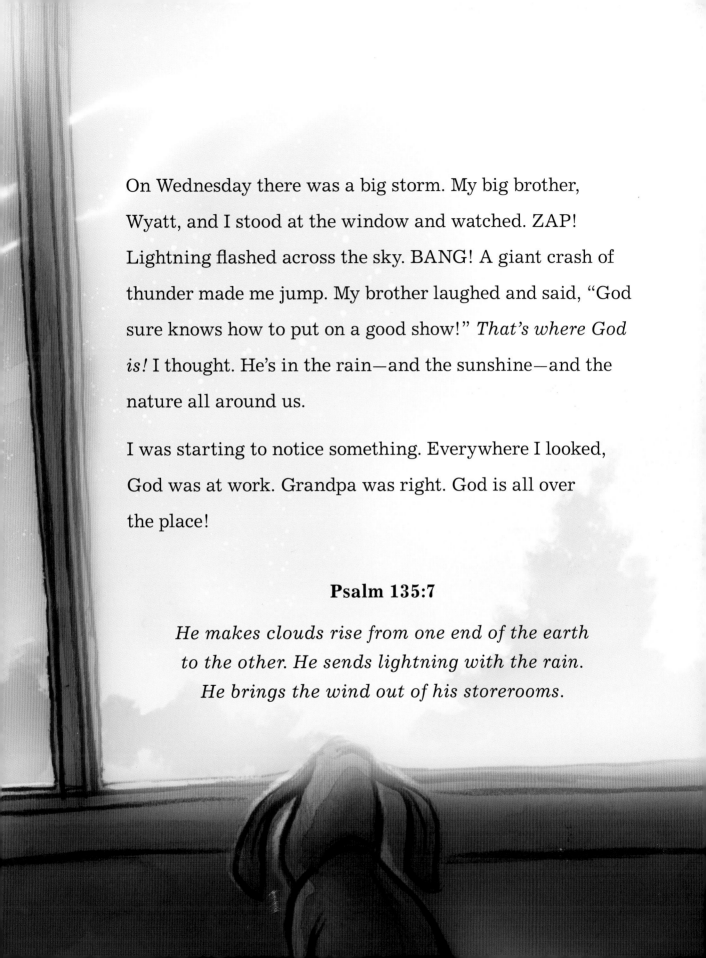

On Wednesday there was a big storm. My big brother, Wyatt, and I stood at the window and watched. ZAP! Lightning flashed across the sky. BANG! A giant crash of thunder made me jump. My brother laughed and said, "God sure knows how to put on a good show!" *That's where God is!* I thought. He's in the rain—and the sunshine—and the nature all around us.

I was starting to notice something. Everywhere I looked, God was at work. Grandpa was right. God is all over the place!

Psalm 135:7

He makes clouds rise from one end of the earth
to the other. He sends lightning with the rain.
He brings the wind out of his storerooms.

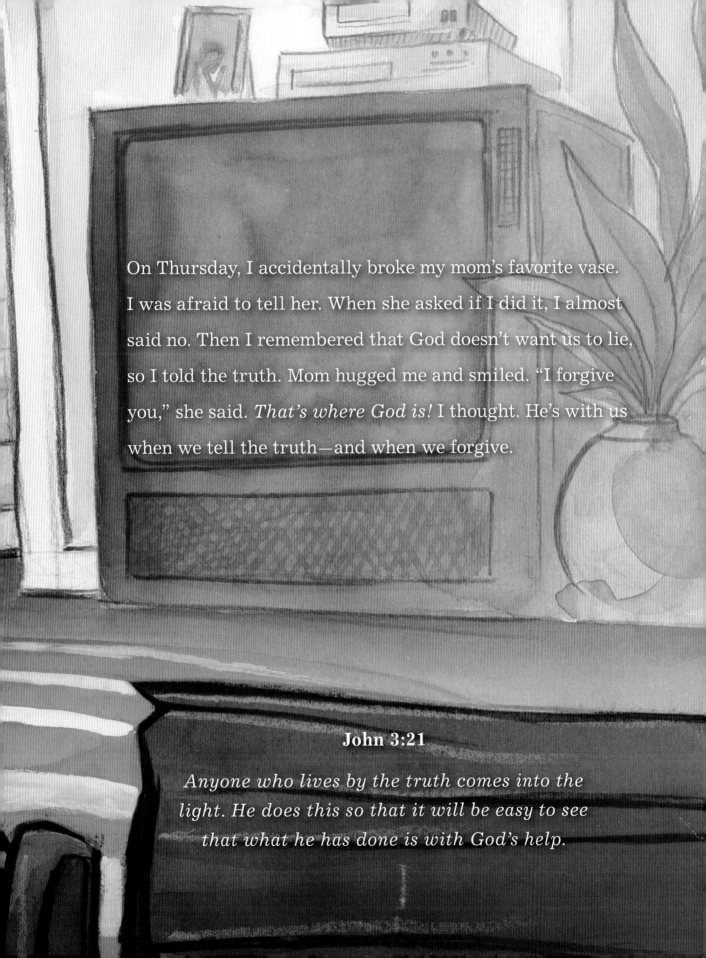

On Thursday, I accidentally broke my mom's favorite vase. I was afraid to tell her. When she asked if I did it, I almost said no. Then I remembered that God doesn't want us to lie, so I told the truth. Mom hugged me and smiled. "I forgive you," she said. *That's where God is!* I thought. He's with us when we tell the truth—and when we forgive.

John 3:21

Anyone who lives by the truth comes into the light. He does this so that it will be easy to see that what he has done is with God's help.

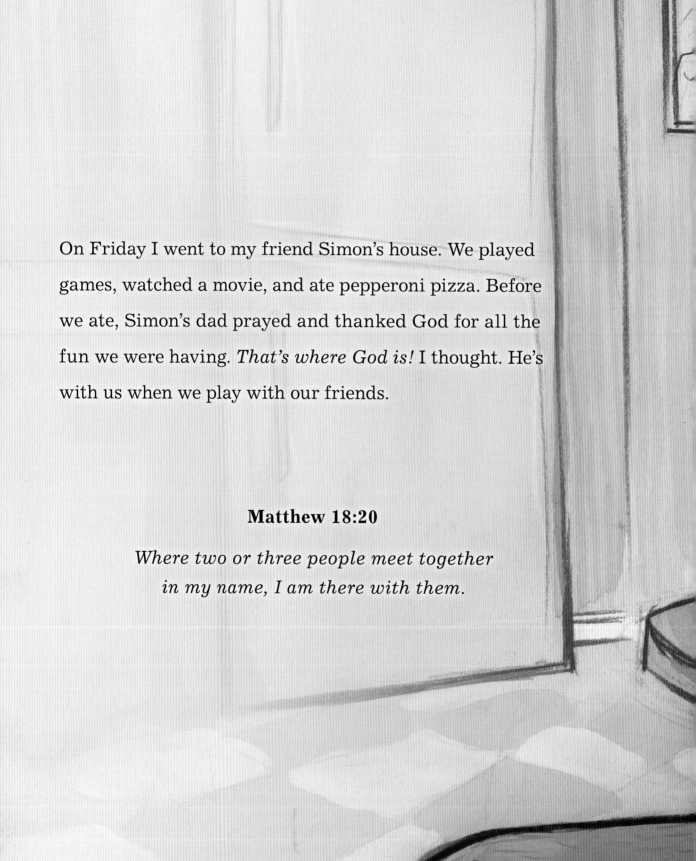

On Friday I went to my friend Simon's house. We played games, watched a movie, and ate pepperoni pizza. Before we ate, Simon's dad prayed and thanked God for all the fun we were having. *That's where God is!* I thought. He's with us when we play with our friends.

Matthew 18:20

*Where two or three people meet together
in my name, I am there with them.*

On Saturday my friends and I were running on the playground. Gavin fell down and scraped his knee. When Abby saw, she pulled Gavin up and brushed him off. *That's where God is!* I thought. He's with us when we help each other.

Proverbs 14:21b

Blessed is the person who is kind to those in need.

On Sunday I went back to Grandpa's house. He picked me up, swung me around, and together we fell into his big comfy chair. "So, did you find God?" he asked.

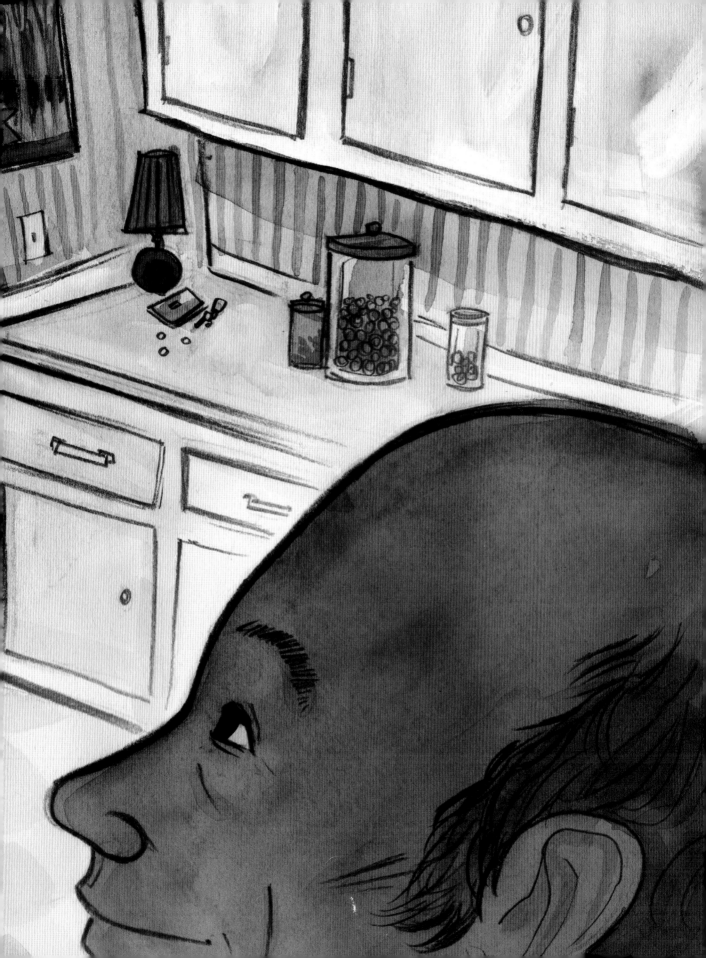

I told Grandpa about all the places I had found God: at the zoo, at the ice cream shop, in the storm, at home, at Simon's house, and on the playground. "Everywhere I go, God is already there!" I said.

Grandpa laughed. "That's true! And there's one more place you can find Him."

"There is?" I asked. "Where else could God be?"

"God can also be in your heart!" Grandpa said with a smile.

"In my heart?" I asked. "How can God be in my heart?"

"You see," said Grandpa, "God wants us to be just like His Son, Jesus. We can't do it on our own, but we can ask God's Spirit to come into our hearts and help us. When we do that we know that God is with us wherever we go."

"That's what I want!" I said. "I want God to be in my heart. I want Him with me wherever I go!"

"Then you should tell Him that," Grandpa said.

"I would love to tell Him, Grandpa, but how?" I asked.

"When we pray, we are talking to God," Grandpa told me. "You can pray to God anytime you want, as much as you want. He will always be listening."

1 John 5:14

There is one thing we can be sure of when we come to God in prayer. If we ask anything in keeping with what he wants, he hears us.

"Can I pray right now, Grandpa?" I wondered.

"You sure can," Grandpa answered. "Just close your eyes, bow your head, and talk to God just like you are talking to me."

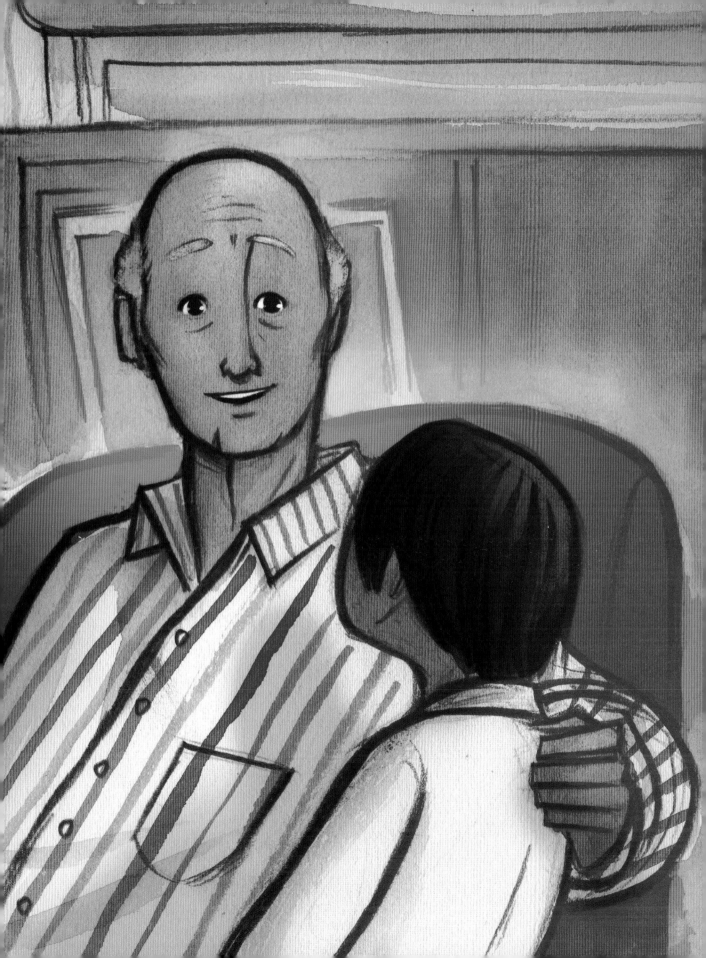

So, I closed my eyes, bowed my head, and started to pray: "Dear God, I am glad that You are all around me. I want You to be with me wherever I go. Come into my heart, and help me to be more like Jesus."

"Amen!" said Grandpa. We got up out of the chair, and Grandpa swung me around and around. Then he pulled me close, gave me a great big hug, and told me that he loved me.

Now I know that it doesn't matter if I'm at home or school, a friend's house or the zoo—or even if I'm all alone somewhere—because wherever I am, that's where God is!

Psalm 139:1–10

Lord, you have seen what is in my heart. You know all about me. You know when I sit down and when I get up. You know what I'm thinking even though you are far away. You know when I go out to work and when I come back home. You know exactly how I live. Lord, even before I speak a word, you know all about it. You are all around me. You are behind me and in front of me. You hold me in your power. I'm amazed at how well you know me. It's more than I can understand. How can I get away from your Spirit? Where can I go to escape from you? If I go up to the heavens, you are there. If I lie down in the deepest parts of the earth, you are also there. Suppose I were to rise with the sun in the east and then cross over to the west where it sinks into the ocean. Your hand would always be there to guide me. Your right hand would still be holding me close.

Dear Parent,

I'll be honest: I get tears in my eyes when I read this tender little book about God. Oh, sure, it's partly because this is such a touching story: A grandpa sends a child out on a mission to discover where God is. The boy not only finds evidence of God in everyday life, but he also takes the further step of inviting Him into his heart so God can be with him forever. When I see the innocence of a child encounter the loving presence of our Creator— well, I can't help but get a little teary.

But that's not the only reason I get emotional. You see, when my daughter was a toddler, she loved to climb into a chair and snuggle as my wife, Leslie, or I would read her a story. But I don't recall many books about God. At the time, Leslie was agnostic and I was an atheist.

Nevertheless, God's love ended up touching our lives, and both Leslie and I became followers of Jesus. By His grace, our daughter, Alison, and her brother, Kyle, found faith, too, and have become strong and vibrant Christians. In fact, guess what Alison has done now? She and her husband, Dan, have created this very book! So today, Leslie and I can pull our little granddaughters onto our laps and read them this story of finding God in the nooks and crannies of daily life—and explain how they, too, can find eternal life through Him.

I know you'll love to read this book to your own children and grandchildren. And when you close the cover, don't let that be the last word. As the grandpa in the story says, "Keep your eyes open. I'm sure you'll find God all over the place." Together, may you and the children in your life joyfully embark on the everyday adventure of discovering God's presence throughout His creation.

— Lee Strobel